A MAGIC CIRCLE BOOK

"WHAT IS IT?"
said the dog.

story by **MARGARET BUELL ALLEN**
pictures by **JUDY SUE GOODWIN**

THEODORE CLYMER
SENIOR AUTHOR, READING 360

GINN AND COMPANY
A XEROX EDUCATION COMPANY

"Look at the funny dog,"
said the dog.

"It is not a dog," said the lion.

4

"But it can go fast like me,"
said the dog.

"You can go fast,
and it can go fast,"
said the lion.
"But it is not a dog."

"Is it a lion?" said the dog.
"It can roar like you."

"I can roar, and it can roar.
But it is not a lion,"
said the lion.

"Can it swim?" said the turtle.

The dog said, "No, it can't swim."

"Well, it can't be a turtle,"
said the turtle.
"I can swim."

"What is it?" said the dog.

"Go and see the hen,"
said the lion.
"She will tell you what it is."

Go
and
see
the
hen ...

The dog ran to look for the hen.

"Hen," said the dog, "did you see
the funny thing?"

"No," said the hen.
"Tell me what it is like."

The dog said, "It can go fast.
But it is not a dog.
It can roar.
But it is not a lion.
It can't swim like a turtle.
What is it?" said the dog.

"Can it fly?" said the hen.

"Yes," said the dog.

"Can it lay eggs?" said the hen.

"No," said the dog.

"Well, it can't be a hen,"
said the hen.
"I can fly, and it can fly.
But I can lay eggs, and it cannot."

The mouse said, "Is the funny thing
little like me?"

"No," said the dog.
"It is big."

"It can go fast, and it can roar.
It is big, and it can fly.
It cannot swim,
and it cannot lay eggs.
Can you guess what it is?"
said the lion.

A Helicopter

16